This book belongs to

....

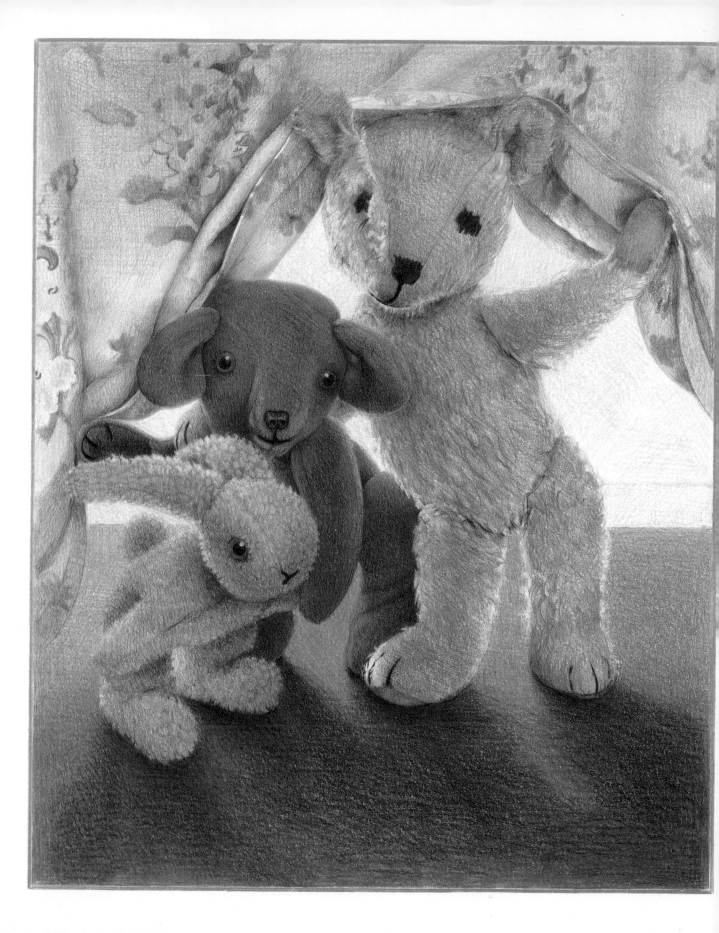

THE
JANE HISSEY
TREASURY

Old Bear

Little Bear's Trousers

Little Bear Lost

WHSMITH
EXCLUSIVE
· BOOKS ·

This edition produced in 1992
exclusively for
WH Smith Limited
Greenbridge Road
Swindon
Wiltshire
SN3 3LD
by Hutchinson Children's Books,
an imprint of the Random Century Group

Old Bear © 1986 Jane Hissey
Little Bear's Trousers © 1987 Jane Hissey
Little Bear Lost © 1989 Jane Hissey

ISBN 0 09 177173 0

Printed in Hong Kong

Old Bear

JANE HISSEY

IT wasn't anybody's birthday, but Bramwell Brown had a feeling that today was going to be a special day. He was sitting thoughtfully on the windowsill with his friends Duck, Rabbit and Little Bear when he suddenly remembered that someone wasn't there who should be.

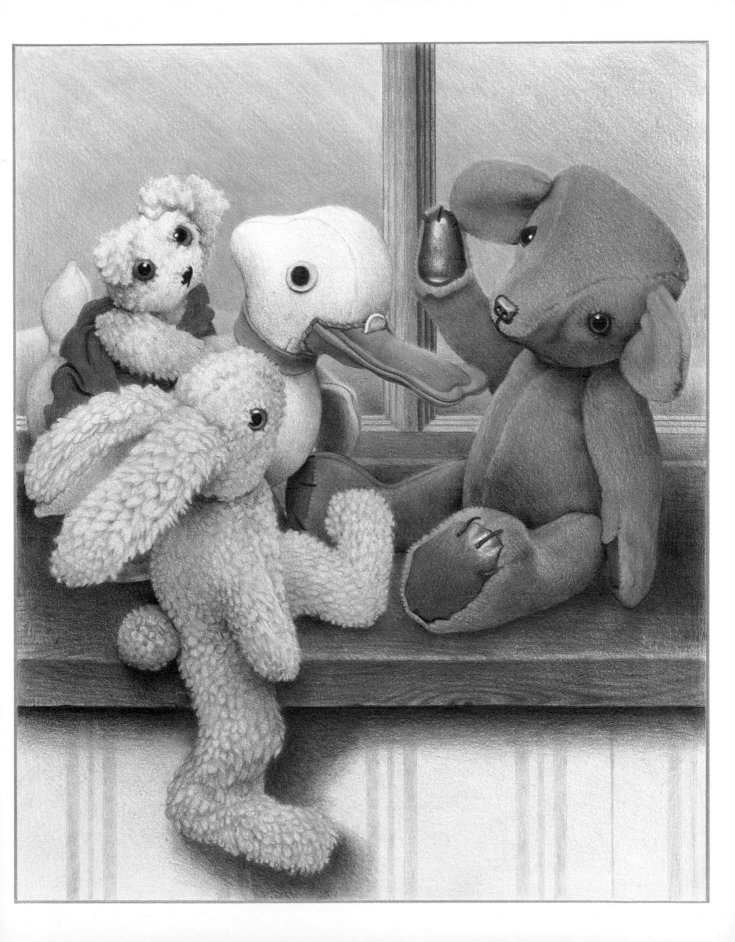

A VERY long time ago, he had seen his good friend Old Bear being packed away in a box. Then he was taken up a ladder, through a trap door and into the attic. The children were being too rough with him and he needed somewhere safe to go for a while.

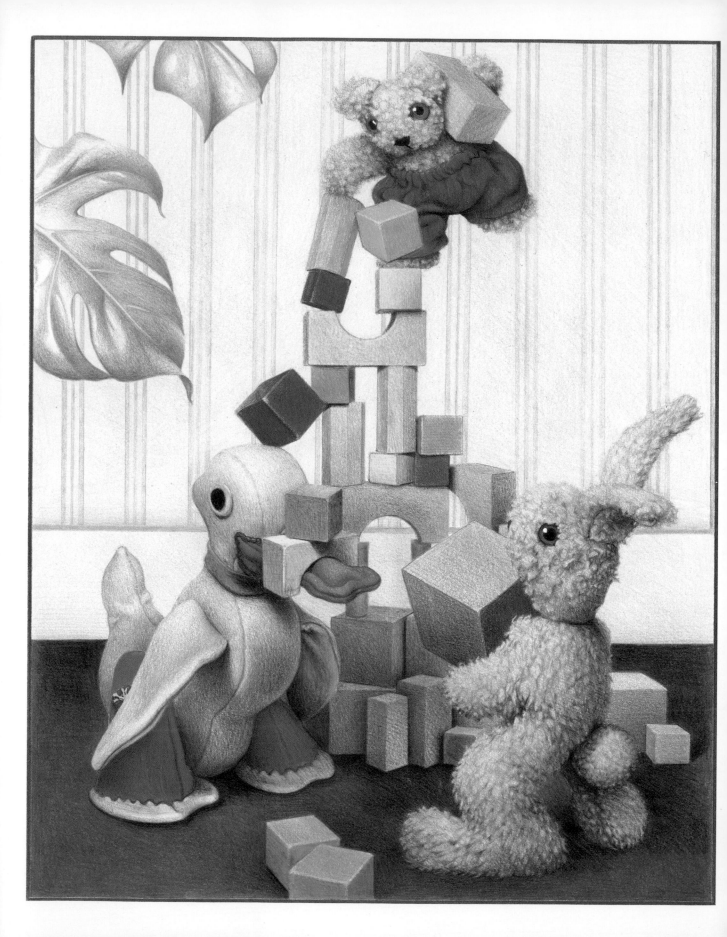

H<small>AS</small> he been forgotten, do you think?' Bramwell asked his friends.

'I think he might have been,' said Rabbit.

'Well,' said Little Bear, 'isn't it time he came back down with us? The children are older now and would look after him properly. Let's go and get him!'

'What a marvellous idea!' said Bramwell. 'But how can we rescue him? It's a long way up to the attic and we haven't got a ladder.'

'We could build a tower of bricks,' suggested Little Bear.

Rabbit collected all the bricks and the others set about building the tower. It grew very tall, and Little Bear was just putting on the last brick when the tower began to wobble.

'Look out!' he cried as the whole thing came tumbling down.

'Never mind,' said Bramwell, helping Little Bear to his feet. 'We'll just have to think of something else.'

LET'S try making *ourselves* into a tower,' said Duck. 'Good idea!' said Bramwell.

Little Bear climbed on top of Rabbit's head and Rabbit hopped onto Duck's beak. They stretched up as far as they could, but then Duck opened his beak to say something, Rabbit wobbled, and they all collapsed on top of Bramwell.

'Sorry,' said Duck, 'perhaps that wasn't a very good idea.'

'Not one of your best,' replied Bramwell from somewhere underneath the heap.

I KNOW!' said Rabbit. 'Let's try bouncing on the bed.'

'Trust you to think of that,' said Bramwell. 'You never can resist a bit of bouncing, especially when it's not allowed.'

Rabbit climbed on to the bed and began to bounce up and down. The others joined him. They bounced higher and higher but *still* they couldn't reach the trap door in the ceiling.

Duck began to cry. 'Oh dear,' he sobbed. 'What are we going to do now? We'll never be able to rescue Old Bear and he'll be stuck up there getting lonelier and lonelier for ever and ever.'

'We mustn't give up,' said Bramwell firmly. 'Come on, Little Bear, you're good at ideas.'

But Little Bear had already noticed the plant in the corner of the room.

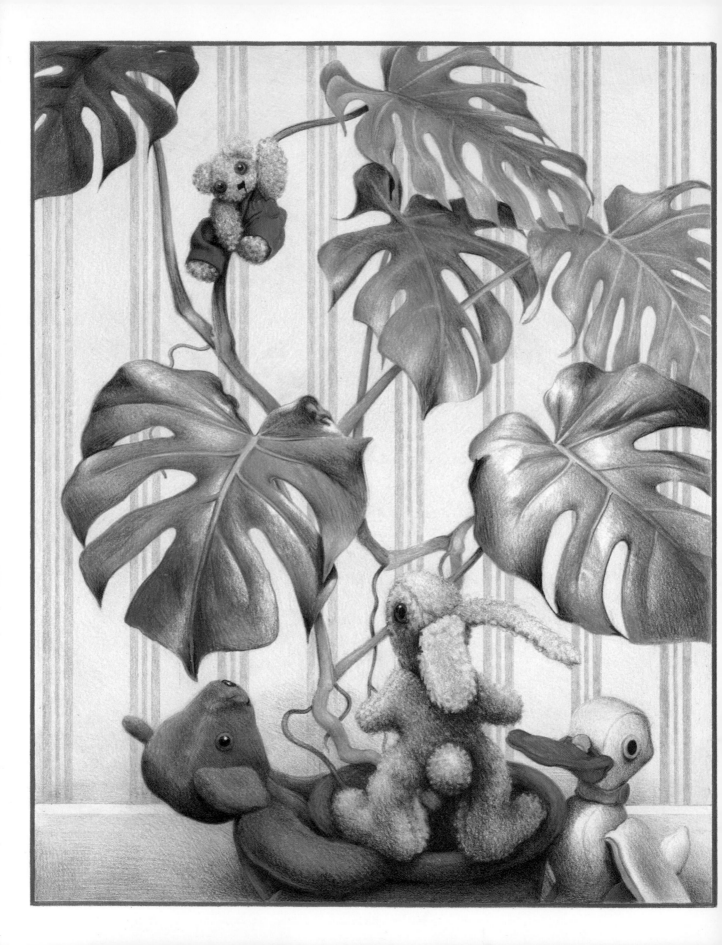

I'VE got it!' he cried. 'I could climb up this plant, swing from the leaves, kick the trap door open and jump in!'

In case it wobbled, Bramwell Brown, Duck and Rabbit steadied the pot. Little Bear bravely climbed up the plant until he reached the very top leaf. He took hold of it and started to swing to and fro, but he swung so hard that the leaf broke and he went crashing down. Luckily, Bramwell Brown was right underneath to catch him in his paws.

'That was a rotten idea,' said Little Bear.

'What I was thinking,' said Duck, 'was that it is a pity I can't fly very well, as I could have been quite a help.'

'Ah ha!' said Bramwell. 'That, my dear Duck, has given me a very good idea. I really think this one might work.'

In the corner of the playroom was a little wooden aeroplane with a propeller that went round and round.

'We could use this plane to get to the trap door,' said Bramwell. 'Rather dangerous, I know, but quite honestly I can't bear to think of Old Bear up there alone for a minute longer.'

'I'll be pilot,' said Rabbit, hopping up and down, making aeroplane noises.

'And I'll stand on the back and push the trap door open with my paintbrush,' said Little Bear.

'But how will you get down?' asked Duck.

'I've already thought of that,' said Bramwell, who hadn't really but quickly did. 'They can use these handkerchiefs as parachutes and we'll catch them in a blanket.'

BRAMWELL gave Little Bear two big handkerchiefs and a torch so he could see into the attic. Then he began to wind up the propeller of the plane. Rabbit and Little Bear climbed aboard and Bramwell began the countdown: 'Five! Four! Three! Two! One! ZERO!'

They were off! The plane whizzed along the carpet and flew up into the air.

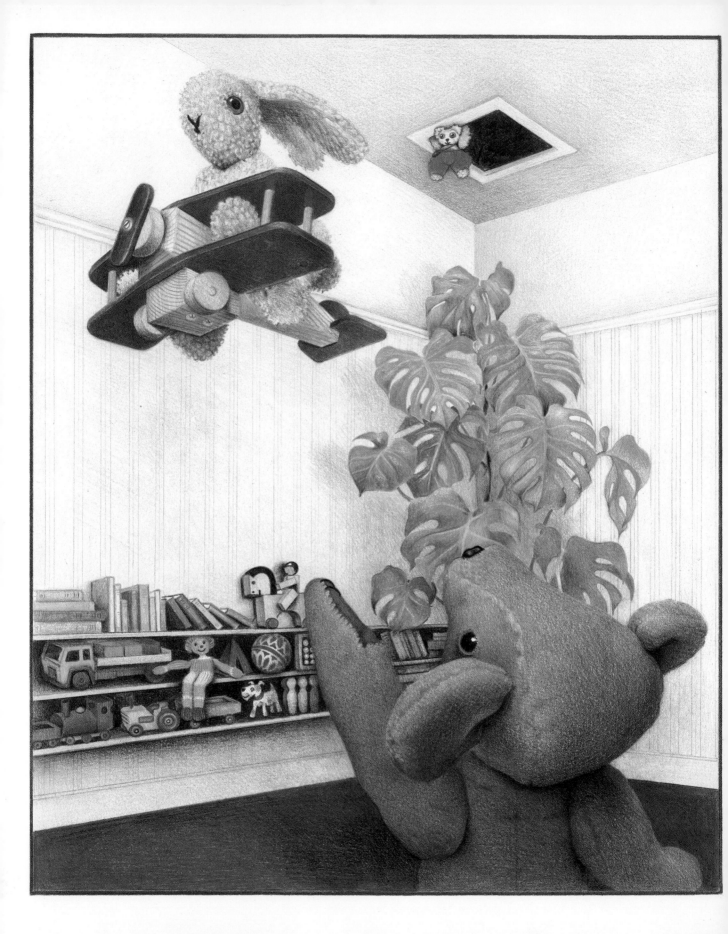

THE little plane flew beautifully and the first time they passed the trap door Little Bear was able to push the lid open with his paintbrush. Then Rabbit circled the plane again, this time very close to the hole. Little Bear grabbed the edge and with a mighty heave he pulled himself inside.

He got out his torch and looked around. The attic was very dark and quiet; full of boxes, old clothes and dust. He couldn't see Old Bear at all.

'Any bears in here?' he whispered, and stood still to listen.

From somewhere quite near he heard a muffled 'Grrrrr,' followed by, 'Did somebody say something?' Little Bear moved a few things aside and there, propped up against a cardboard box and covered in dust, was Old Bear.

LITTLE Bear jumped up and down with excitement. 'Old Bear! Old Bear! I've found Old Bear!' he shouted.

'So you have,' said Old Bear.

'Have you been lonely?' asked Little Bear.

'Quite lonely,' said Old Bear. 'But I've been asleep a lot of the time.'

'Well,' said Little Bear kindly, 'would you like to come back to the playroom with us now?'

'That would be lovely,' replied Old Bear. 'But how will we get down?'

'Don't worry about that,' said Little Bear, 'Bramwell has thought of everything. He's given us these handkerchiefs to use as parachutes.'

'G ood old Bramwell,' said the old teddy. 'I'm glad he didn't forget me.' Old Bear stood up and shook the dust out of his fur and Little Bear helped him into his parachute. They went over to the hole in the ceiling.

'Ready,' shouted Rabbit.
'Steady,' shouted Duck.
'GO!' shouted Bramwell Brown.

The two bears leapt bravely from the hole in the ceiling. Their handkerchief parachutes opened out and they floated gently down . . . landing safely in the blanket.

WELCOME home, Old Bear,' said Bramwell
Brown, patting his friend on the back.
The others patted him too, just to make him feel
at home. 'It's nice to have you back,' they said.
'It's nice to *be* back,' replied Old Bear.

THAT night, when all the animals were tucked up in bed, Bramwell thought about the day's adventures and looked at the others.

Rabbit was dreaming exciting dreams about bouncing as high as an aeroplane.

Duck was dreaming that he could really fly and was rescuing bears from all sorts of high places.

Little Bear was dreaming of all the interesting things he had seen in the attic, and Old Bear was dreaming about the good times he would have now he was back with his friends.

'I *knew* it was going to be a special day,' said Bramwell Brown to himself.

JANE HISSEY

Little Bear's Trousers

THE sun shone through the window and woke Little Bear. 'What a lovely morning,' he said to himself. 'I'll do something different today.'

HE jumped down from the bed, took off his pyjamas and looked for his trousers.

He looked on the chair where he'd left them and he looked on the floor under the chair – and then he looked through the chest of drawers in case they were there. But they weren't. They were nowhere.

'But they must be somewhere,' said Little Bear. 'Trousers don't disappear. I'll go and ask Old Bear. *He'll* know where they are.'

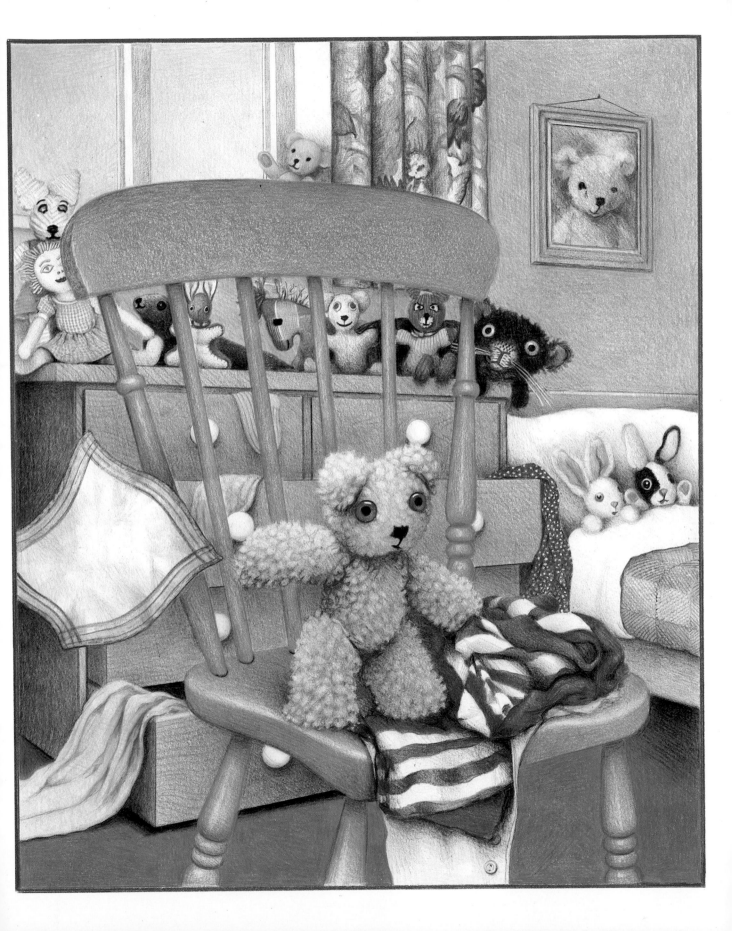

OLD Bear was already enjoying the sun in his deckchair. 'I haven't seen your trousers, I'm afraid,' he said. 'But Camel was around here earlier. Perhaps she knows where they are.'

OH dear,' said Camel, when Little Bear found her a few minutes later. 'I did find them. I thought they were a pair of hump warmers and I tried them on to see if they fitted me. They did keep my humps *quite* warm but the air came down the tops so I decided these were better.' And she showed Little Bear two very smart bobble hats – one for each hump.

'I gave the old hump warmers to Sailor to use as sails for his boat. Jump on my back and let's see if we can find him.' Little Bear scrambled up and they galloped off in the direction of the bathroom.

SAILOR was looking after the boats and ducks in the bathroom. 'I did use them as sails,' he said, 'but they looked too much like trousers.'

'That's because they *are* trousers,' said Little Bear crossly. 'Where are they now?'

'I gave them to Dog to keep his bones in,' said Sailor. 'Sorry, Little Bear. We'd better hurry, he might be anywhere by now.'

D OG was happily burying his bones in flowerpots when Little Bear found him. 'My bones kept falling through the two-bone bone-holder,' he said.

'TWO-BONE BONE-HOLDER!' cried Little Bear in dismay. 'Oh, Dog, can't you recognize trousers when you see them?'

'Oh, dear,' said Dog. 'I do feel silly. I gave them to Rabbit – he said he needed a skiing hat, and your trousers looked just perfect. I am sorry.'

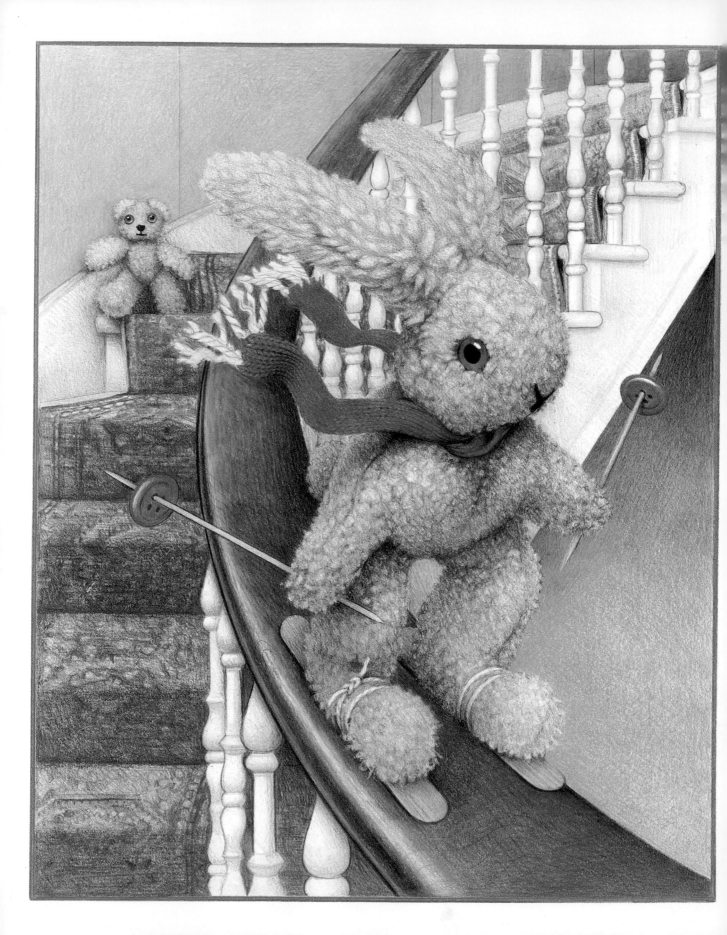

WHEEE!' cried Rabbit, as he shot past Little Bear a few minutes later, skiing down the bannister on two lolly stick skis. He didn't have Little Bear's trousers on his head now.

'But I did have them earlier,' he explained when Little Bear caught up with him. 'They made a lovely rabbit hat, with plenty of room for my ears. But they slipped over my eyes and I crashed, so I decided it was safer without them. I gave them to Zebra to carry her building bricks in.'

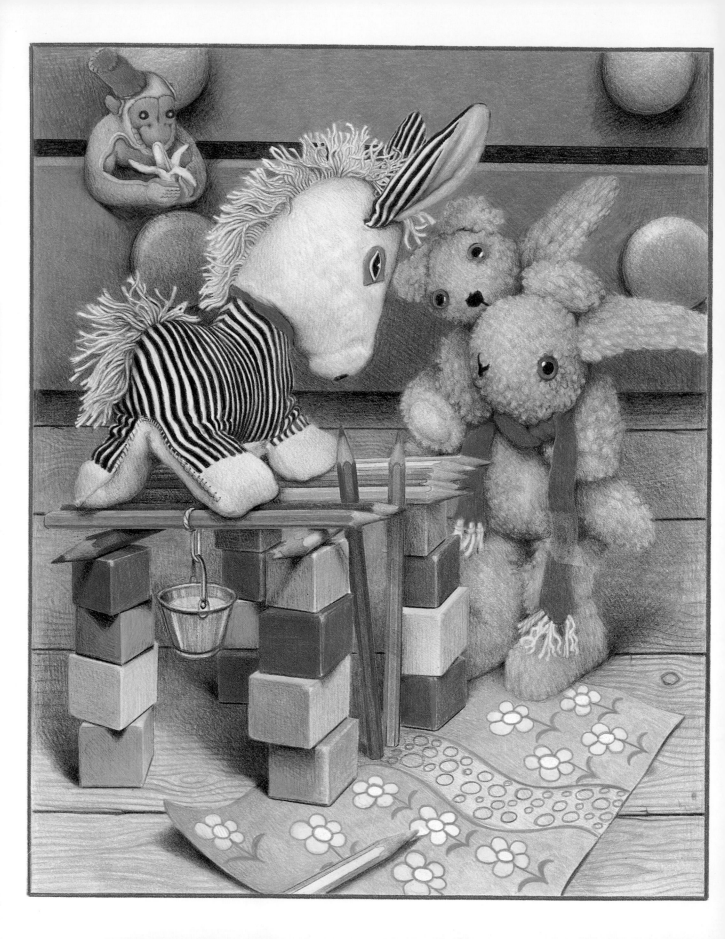

ZEBRA was building herself a house when Little Bear arrived. But his trousers were nowhere to be seen.

'I wondered whose they were,' she said. 'They were terribly useful. I tied up the legs with string, put them on my back and carried all these bricks here in them. But when I had enough bricks for my house I gave them to Duck to use as a flag for his sand castle. I am sorry, Little Bear. I didn't know they belonged to you.'

D UCK was in the sand tray looking sadly at the castle he'd made. There was no trouser flag on the top now. 'I did use the flag that Zebra gave me,' he sighed. 'But Bramwell Brown came and said it was just what he needed, urgently, in the kitchen. He gave me this paper flag to use instead.'

'Never mind,' said Little Bear with a sigh, feeling quite glad that his trousers were not covered in sand.

The kitchen was in a terrible muddle. There were bowls and spoons and eggs and flour, and in the middle of it all sat Bramwell Brown.

HE had Little Bear's trousers but, oh dear, he'd
filled them with pink icing and was busy
decorating a huge cake with them.

'It's a special occasion cake,' said Bramwell. 'And
you have to put icing on special occasion cakes. I
thought I could do two stripes at once with these
icing bags.'

'But they're *not* icing bags. They are my trousers!'
sniffed Little Bear, trying hard not to cry.

'I thought I'd seen them before,'
said Bramwell Brown.

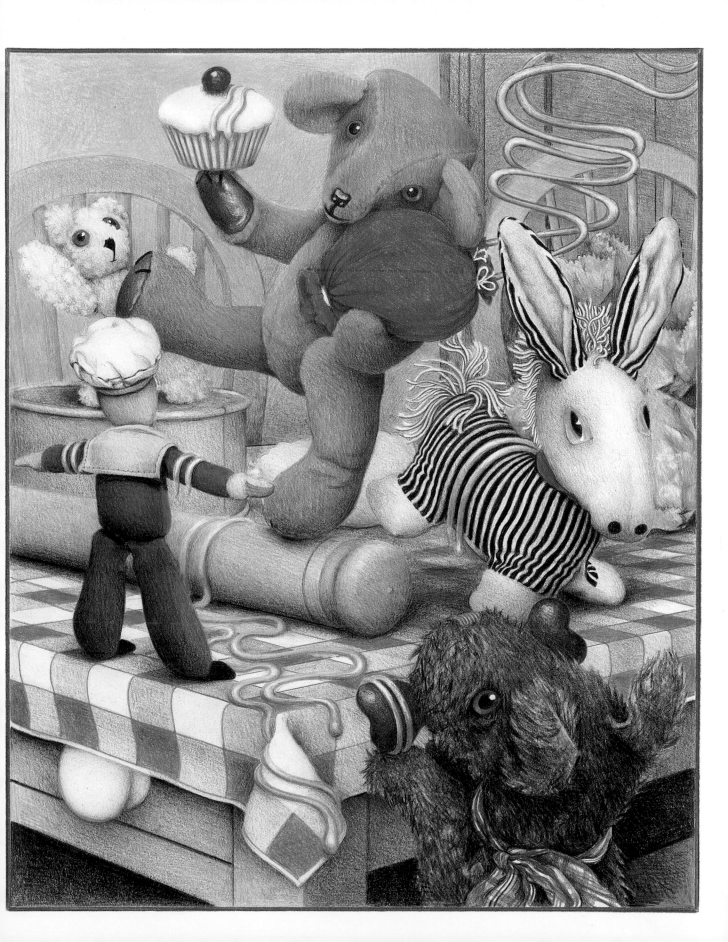

DON'T worry, Little Bear,' said Old Bear, who always arrived at the right moment. 'The icing will wash out and they'll look as good as new.'

'What's the special occasion cake for?' asked Little Bear, feeling a bit more cheerful at this news.

'Well, I didn't really know,' said Bramwell. 'I just felt like making one.'

Old Bear thought hard, 'Perhaps it ought to be a Trousers Day Cake,' he suggested helpfully.

So that's what Bramwell Brown wrote on the cake. Twice. Once with the icing from the left trouser leg and once with the icing from the right trouser leg. It said, Happy Trousers Day, in the middle, and there was a trousers pattern all round the edge.

DUCK washed Little Bear's trousers and dried them next to the cooker. Then all the toys sat down to enjoy a piece of cake and to celebrate the day Little Bear lost, and found, his trousers.

AND ever since Trousers Day, Little Bear has slept with his trousers under his pillow. 'Nobody will find them there,' he says.

JANE HISSEY

Little Bear Lost

OLD Bear had been busy all morning. He'd packed an enormous picnic for all the toys. There were sandwiches, cakes, buns, pies and jellies.

'I think I've put in a bit too much food,' he said to himself as he sat on the picnic-basket lid to try to make it close.

Suddenly in a blur of fur and red trousers, Little Bear dashed past the basket and dived into a heap of books. 'Do you think anyone will find me?' he asked from the middle of the heap.

'I shouldn't think so,' said Old Bear. 'Who's looking for you?'

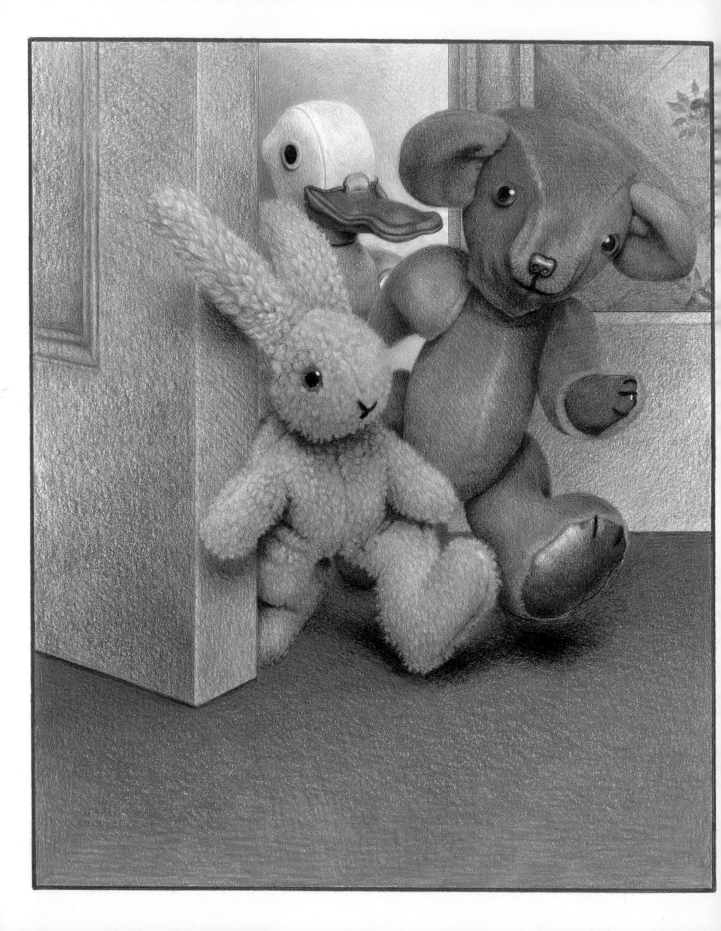

Bᴜᴛ before Little Bear could answer, the door flew open and into the room ran Bramwell Brown, Duck and Rabbit. They didn't seem to be looking for Little Bear and, in a moment, they were hiding too. Rabbit and Duck were behind the curtains and Bramwell's feet could just be seen sticking out from under a cushion.

'We're playing hide and seek,' explained the cushion in a Bramwell Brown sort of voice. 'Did anyone see us hide?'

'Only me,' said Old Bear, 'but who's looking for you?'

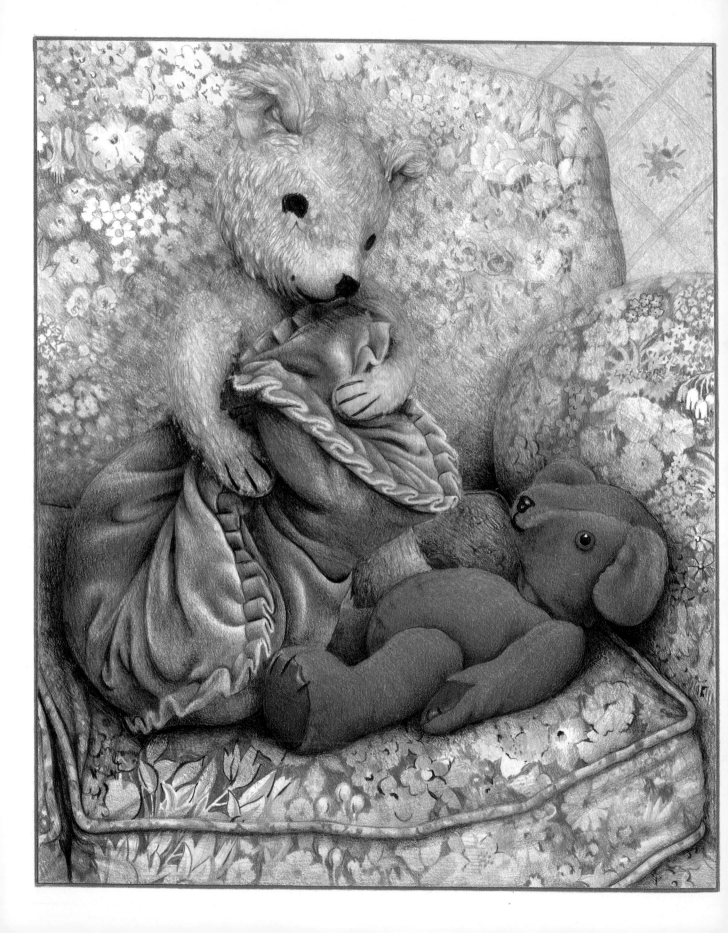

THERE was a bit of a silence and then the cushion moved.

Bramwell looked sadly up at Old Bear. 'Oh dear,' he said, miserably, 'we've done it again. We've forgotten to have a seeker in our game of hide-and-seek.'

The others crept out of their hiding places and sat down on Bramwell's cushion.

'What a pity,' said Duck. 'It could have been a good game, too.'

'Old Bear,' said Little Bear, thoughtfully, 'if we all hide again, could you look for us?'

O LD Bear said that was a good idea and, with paws over his eyes, he slowly counted to ten.

'One, two, three,' he began, as Rabbit jumped into a vase and tried to look like a bunch of flowers.

'Four, five, six,' he continued, as Duck jumped into a shoe box.

'Seven, eight, nine,' he said, giving Bramwell time to hide a last bit of paw.

'TEN,' he called; 'I'm READY!' And by then Little Bear had also disappeared.

O LD Bear looked all around the room to see
whether any paws or ears were showing. It
wasn't very tidy.

First he found a sock that he'd lost weeks ago. And
then he found at least ten marbles that had rolled
underneath things. He even found Cat, who wasn't
really lost or hiding, and Cat helped him look for the
others. But he couldn't find them.

'It's no good,' he sighed. 'I can't find any of you. I
can only find things I'm *not* looking for. Can we tidy
up a bit and then start again?'

ONE by one the other toys wriggled out of their secret hiding places. All of them, that is, except Little Bear.

'Where's Little Bear?' asked Bramwell Brown, but nobody seemed to know.

'Well he can't be far away,' said Old Bear. 'Let's give him a shout.'

They all climbed up on a chair and called 'LITTLE BEAR' so loudly that they made themselves jump and almost fell off. Duck prodded all the cushions with his beak to see whether Little Bear was underneath, and Bramwell peered under the bed.

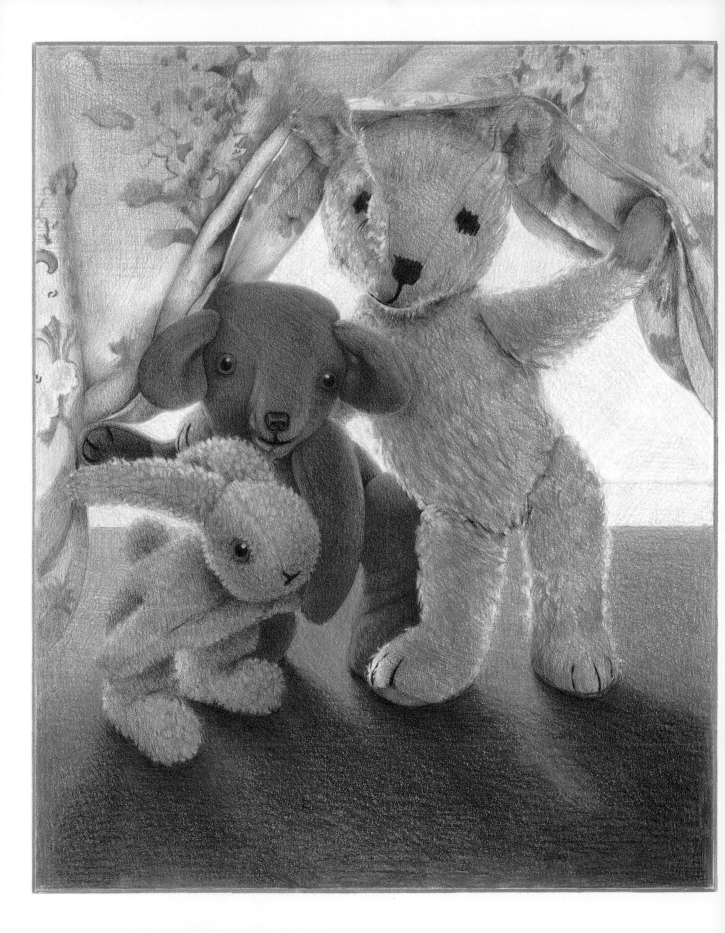

HE could be under here,' he said.
'Well, I'm not going to look,' said Duck. 'It's
dark and dusty.'

'Oh, I'll go,' said Rabbit. 'It's just like a tunnel and
I love tunnels.' He was just about to dive under the
bed when Bramwell grabbed him by the tail.

'Wait a minute, Rabbit,' he said. 'I'll give you the
end of this string and then you won't get lost
because we'll all be on the other end.'

WITH the string tied round his middle, Rabbit bounded into the darkness. The others waited and watched.

Suddenly the string gave such a jerk that Duck fell on his beak.

'He's here, he's here!' squeaked Rabbit. 'I'm holding on to him, can you pull us out?'

All together they pulled hard on the string and out popped Rabbit, tail first, clutching not Little Bear but . . .

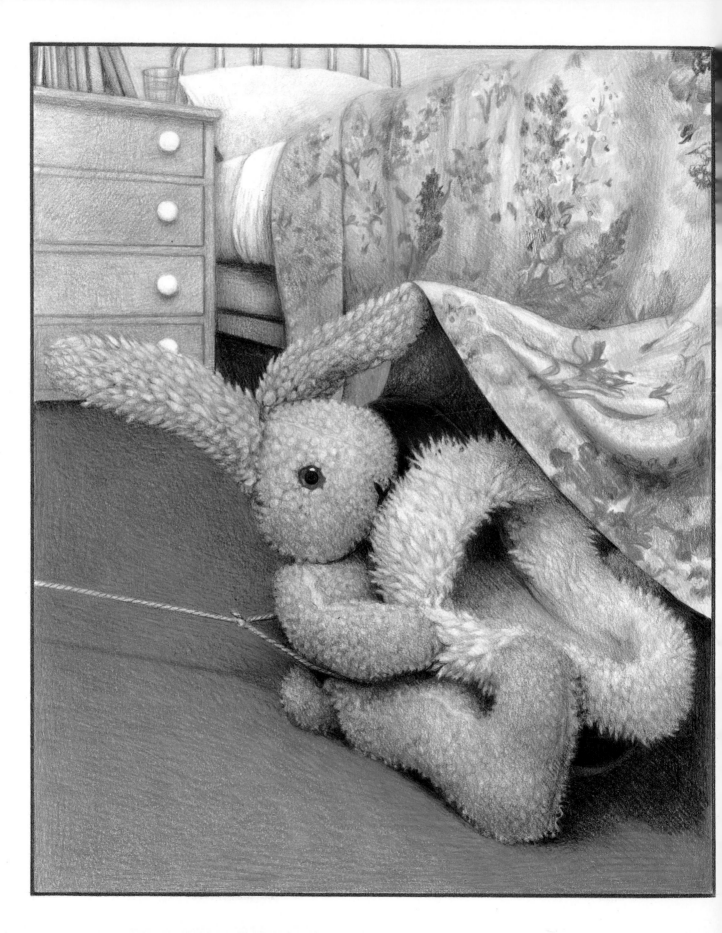

. . . a fluffy slipper!

'Oh,' said Duck, looking down at the slipper, 'I don't think that's Little Bear.'

'Of course it's not,' said Bramwell. 'He never looked like that.'

'It *felt* like Little Bear,' said Rabbit.

'It's not your fault, Rabbit,' said Old Bear, kindly. 'You were very brave to go in there on your own and I'm sure Little Bear will turn up soon.'

'I bet he won't,' said Duck, still gazing at the slipper. 'He's probably wandered off and is miles away by now.'

'Rubbish!' said Bramwell. 'I expect he's just stuck in something. We must keep looking.'

I think we should make a poster saying "This bear is lost", with a picture of Little Bear on it,' said Old Bear. 'Then all the toys will know who we're looking for.'

The animals all fetched the painting things and Bramwell sat and painted a picture of a small bear in red trousers that did look quite a bit like Little Bear. There wasn't really enough room to write 'This bear is lost', so they just made him look a bit sad and hoped that everyone would know what it meant.

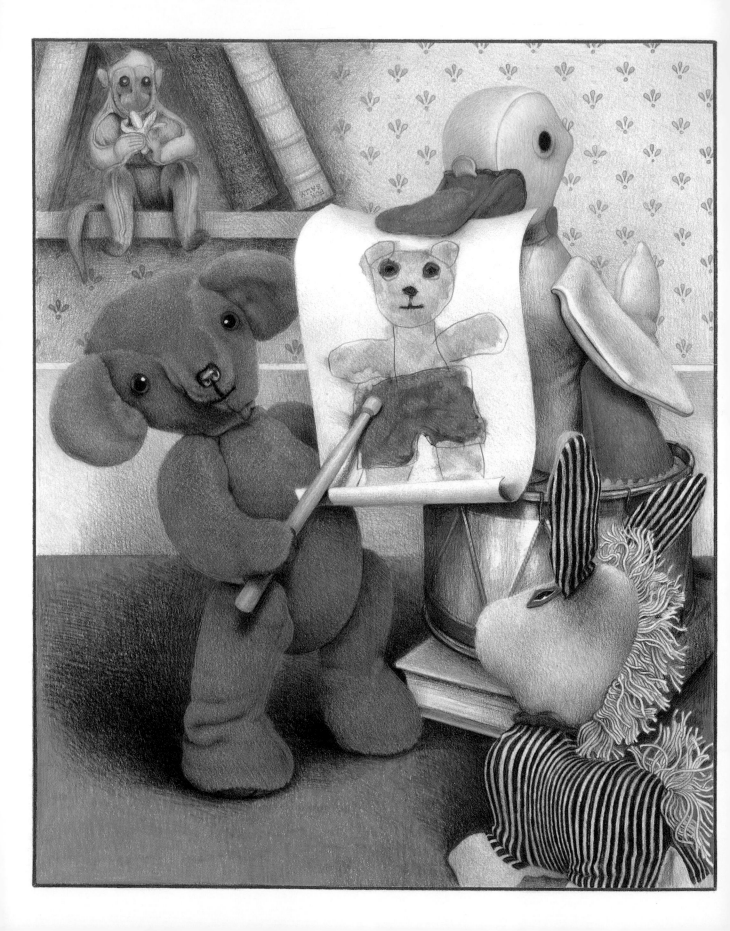

JUST to make sure, Bramwell called all the other toys together and explained what had happened. They all wanted to help and, within minutes, everyone was searching.

They rolled up rugs and climbed up curtains. They jumped into drawers and turned out toys. They peered behind plants and rummaged through rubbish.

They felt as though they'd searched through the whole house but still there was no sign of Little Bear.

PHEW, I'm tired,' said Bramwell Brown.

'And I'm hungry,' said Duck.

'Well,' said Old Bear, 'everyone has worked very hard and I think we all deserve our picnic. When we've eaten we'll start looking again.'

He led the way to the picnic basket that he'd packed in the morning and lifted the lid.

'There,' he said proudly. 'What do you think of that?'

THE animals all peered inside. But what they saw was not what they had expected to see.

There, lying tucked up under a tea cloth, fast asleep and looking very full, was Little Bear.

'Well, well!' gasped Bramwell Brown.

'Hmm, we seem to have found a bear and lost a picnic,' said Duck, staring at the crumbs that covered Little Bear.

'It's a good thing I made too much then,' said Old Bear. 'There's still plenty left for us.'

Bramwell Brown lifted Little Bear out of the basket and gave him a big hug.

'Come on everyone,' he called, 'picnic time!'

CAREFULLY, they dragged the basket bumpety bump down the stairs and out into the garden.

'This looks like a good place for a picnic,' said Old Bear, spreading the cloth out under a tree.

They had a wonderful feast, finishing every crumb in the basket. Then they stretched out in the sun to rest.

'I know,' said Little Bear, suddenly leaping to his feet, 'let's have *another* game of hide-and-seek.'

But there was no reply. Leaning against the tree and full of food, all the other toys were fast asleep.

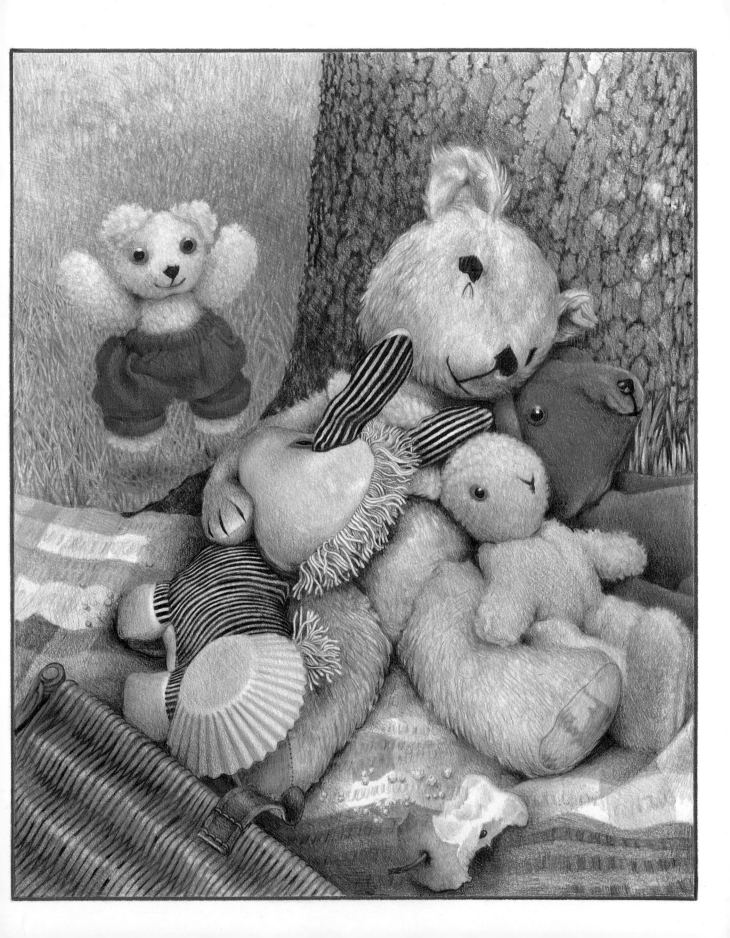